This book belongs to

....

....

For Hugh Lebihan Lowther
K.L.

For Martha & Lucille
D.A.

EGMONT
We bring stories to life

First published in Great Britain 2013
by Egmont UK Limited
The Yellow Building, 1 Nicholas Road, London W11 4AN
www.egmont.co.uk

Text copyright © Kara Lebihan 2013
Illustrations copyright © Deborah Allwright 2013

The moral rights of the author and illustrator have been asserted.

ISBN 978 1 4052 5395 6 (Paperback)
ISBN 978 1 7803 1340 5 (Ebook)

A CIP catalogue record for this title is available from the British Library.

MRS VICKERS' KNICKERS

Kara
Lebihan

Deborah
Allwright

EGMONT

Mrs Vickers was just pegging a pretty pair
of knickers on the line when . . .

"My favourite knickers!"

oosh!

Well, that's the end of those, she thought.

But Mrs Vickers was wrong.
That was just the start!

Mrs Vickers' favourite knickers
twisted and twirled on the breeze.

High over the rooftops . . .

. . . far above the town
for **everyone** to see.

They tangled
with a kite . . .

. . . causing quite a display.

Then on they sailed . . .

Over the building site.

Above the town square.

And off down
the High Street.

They
tangled
with some
traffic lights, causing
quite a commotion!

Until an
inquisitive bird
stopped by . . .

. . . and off
flapped
Mrs Vickers'
favourite knickers!

Past the church.

Through the classroom.

Past the zoo.

Round and round and round the rollercoaster.

And into first place!

Then one more gust of wind
and off they went . . .

. . . far away into the distance.

And that really **did** seem to be the end
of Mrs Vickers' favourite knickers.

Until....

BIFF!

They twisted and twirled
all the way back . . . .

. . . to a very
grateful Mrs Vickers.

And that really **did** seem to be the *very* end
of Mrs Vickers' knickers.

Or **was** it?

whooooooosh!